The Earth and the Sky

First Steck-Vaughn Edition 1992

This edition first published in 1987 by Raintree Publishers Inc., a Division of Steck-Vaughn Company.

Text copyright © 1987 by Raintree Publishers Inc.
© 1981 Hachette

All rights reserved. No part of the material protected by this copyright may be reproduced or utilized in any form by any means, electronic or mechanical, including photocopying, recording, or by any information storage and retrieval system, without permission in writing from Steck-Vaughn Company, P.O. Box 26015, Austin, TX 78755. Printed in the United States of America.

Library of Congress Number: 86-33852

2 3 4 5 6 7 8 9   94 93 92

Library of Congress Cataloging in Publication Data

Avérous, Pierre.
　Ask about the earth and the sky.

　Translation of: En regardant le ciel et la terre.
　Summary: Questions and answers present information about the weather, the earth, and the sky.
　1. Weather—Juvenile literature. 2. Earth—Juvenile literature. 3. Sky—Juvenile literature.
[1. Earth. 2. Sky. 3. Weather. 4. Questions and answers] I. Raintree Publishers. II. Title.
QC981.3.E513   1987   551.5   86-33852
ISBN 0-8172-2876-4 (lib. bdg.)
ISBN 0-8172-2888-8 (softcover)

Cover illustration: David Schweitzer

Ask About
The Earth and the Sky

RSVP
RAINTREE
STECK-VAUGHN
PUBLISHERS
The Steck-Vaughn Company

Austin, Texas

Contents

The weather

What is the wind? 8
What makes the wind? 8
What are clouds made of? 10
Where does the water in the clouds come from? 10
How do clouds move? 10
What is a cloud of smoke? 12
Why is there steam over a bath? 12
Why are windows sometimes covered with steam? 12
Why are most clouds white? 14
Why are there pink clouds? 14
Why are there black clouds? 14
Why does it rain? 16
Why does it snow? 16
Why are mountains covered with snow? 16
What is lightning? 18
Why does lightning strike? 18
What makes thunder? 18
How do people forecast the weather? 20
Where does rainwater go? 20
Why do we get dry in the sun? 20
Why does the sun shine so brilliantly? 22
Where do rainbows come from? 22
Where do rainbows go when you don't see them? 22
Why is the sky blue? 24
Why are faraway mountains blue? 24
Why is the sun sometimes red? 24

The earth

Where did the earth come from? 26
Have there always been people on earth? 26
Are there a lot of countries in the world? 28
How do you know when you have gone from one country to another or from one state to another? 28
Is it easy to go from one country or state to another? 28
What is a continent? 30
Are there countries where nobody lives? 30
Are there still unknown countries? 30
What shape is the earth? 32
Why can't I see that the earth is round? 32
Is there an underside to the earth? 32
How does the earth stay in the sky? 34
Could the earth ever fall down? 34
Are there other earths in the sky? 34
How do I stay on the ground? 36
How do birds stay in the sky? 36
How do soap bubbles stay in the air? 36
What is it like at the center of the earth? 38
Are there caves that reach the center of the earth? 38
Can I dig a hole to the center of the earth? 38
Is it true that the earth turns like a top? 40
Will the earth ever stop turning? 40
If the earth is turning, why don't I feel dizzy? 40

The sky

How do airplanes fly? 42
Does the sky touch the earth? 42
Are there any mountains higher than the sky? 44

What is beyond the sky? 44
Can the sky fall down? 44
Where does the sun go when it sets? 46
How does night come? 46
Does the night pass quickly? 46
Why does the sun give us light? 48
What is the sun like? 48
Can the sun be put out? 48
What is a full moon? 50
Why does the moon change its shape? 50
Which is bigger, the moon or the sun? 50
Do clouds touch the moon? 52
Can airplanes fly to the moon? 52
Can rockets go to the moon? 52
What is it like inside a spaceship? 54
Why must astronauts wear special clothing? 54
Why do astronauts float in space? 54
What is the man in the moon? 56
Are there mountains on the moon? 56
Are there any plants on the moon? 56
What are stars? 58
Do stars disappear during the day? 58
Can we ever reach the stars? 58

Glossary 60
Index 62

The weather

What is the wind? The wind cannot be seen. It is invisible. You know it is there when it blows dust, leaves, or your hair. The wind is a huge current of air that blows through the city and country. It blows at sea, over deserts, and in many other places on earth.

What makes the wind? During the daytime, the sun warms the air. The heat from chimneys also warms the air. When air is warmed, it becomes light and rises. Cool air rushes in to replace it. This movement makes the wind.

What are clouds made of?

If you could walk through a big round cloud, you would get wet because it is full of drops of water. In long thin clouds, you would freeze because they are made of specks of ice. In the middle of clouds are strong currents of air that blow in all directions.

Where does the water in the clouds come from?

When it is hot, many little drops of water enter the atmosphere from lakes, rivers, ponds, and so on. The wind takes them everywhere throughout the sky. When lots of them are in one place and it is cold, the little drops of water join together to make bigger drops. These bigger drops make up the clouds.

How do clouds move?

Sometimes we can see clouds moving across the sky. The wind blows them along. Not only does the wind blow through city streets and in the country, it also blows high in the sky.

What is a cloud of smoke?

Although we refer to it as a cloud of smoke, smoke isn't really a cloud at all. A real cloud is full of drops of water and has no smell. Smoke is dirty air that doesn't smell nice and makes us cough. It looks like a cloud because it is light and spreads out like one.

Why is there steam over a bath?

Tiny drops are always escaping from water into the air especially when the water is hot. When the drops rise, they cool and join together to make drops big enough to be seen. This is the steam that you see over a bath.

Why are windows sometimes covered with steam?

There are always many invisible little drops of water in the air. These become bigger drops in areas where it is cold. Put your hand on a window. It feels cold, doesn't it? When many of the invisible drops of water in the warm air inside touch the cold glass, they join to make bigger drops. This is the steam you see on windows.

Why are most clouds white?

Clouds look like soft white cotton, but they are really made of water or ice. When sunlight enters a cloud, the light is reflected by all these drops of water or specks of ice, and the cloud appears white.

Why are there pink clouds?

The drops of water and specks of ice in clouds take on the color of the light that shines on them. At sunset when the light is pink, you see pink clouds.

Why are there black clouds?

Before big storms, the sky becomes very dark. The clouds are so big and thick that the sun cannot shine through them. They look black because they are not lit up. There is no such thing as black light. Black is what you see when there is no light at all.

Why does it rain?

The wind blows in the middle of clouds and stops the little drops of water from falling. Instead, they spin around, rise and fall, and rise again. When they bump into one another, they join together and become bigger. When the clouds grow too big and heavy, the wind cannot keep them high in the sky, and the drops of water fall to the ground as rain.

Why does it snow?

In winter, puddles of water freeze and change to ice. Sometimes the air is so cold in the sky that the tiny drops of water in the clouds freeze. They join together to make snowflakes. When they are too heavy to stay in the sky, the flakes fall to the ground.

Why are mountains covered with snow?

The higher you go up a mountain, the colder it is. Because of the cold, it doesn't rain, it snows, even in summer. The snow on high mountains never melts because the air is always cold. The mountains are covered with snow all year long.

What is lightning? The flashes of lightning in the sky during a storm are giant sparks of electricity. Usually you can't see electricity. When the weather is bad, however, electricity moves across the sky in zigzags that can be seen. It can go anywhere it wishes, unlike the electricity directed into homes through electrical wires.

Why does lightning strike? Lightning sometimes strikes the earth during a storm. It is attracted by steeples, trees, towers, or anything that is tall and pointed. Sometimes there are lightning conductors on the roofs of tall buildings which stop the lightning from doing any harm. It is best to stay indoors during a thunderstorm. Never hide under a tree during a storm because the tree may be struck by lightning.

What makes thunder? When a flash of lightning crosses the sky, the air parts quickly to let it through. This quick movement of air makes a loud noise which is called thunder. Thunder isn't dangerous. Although it sounds very frightening, it is just a noise.

How do people forecast the weather?

Meteorologists use special instruments to predict the weather. The information that they have gathered is then broadcast over radio and television or printed in newspapers. Forecasting is very difficult, so the weather forecast may not always be correct.

Where does rainwater go?

After a rainstorm in the city, the water drains off the streets and runs into large pipes called sewers which are under the ground. The sewers carry the water to rivers or to the sea. When it rains in the country, the water runs over the ground into streams, rivers, and the sea. Some of it soaks slowly into the earth or evaporates.

Why do we get dry in the sun?

After swimming, you can lie in the sun to get dry without getting cold. The sun is like a huge lamp that warms you. The water warms on your skin and evaporates, and you are dry.

21

Why does the sun shine so brilliantly?

Sunlight is made up of all the colors of the rainbow—red, orange, yellow, green, blue, indigo, and violet. When these colors are all mixed together, they make white. This is why the sun seems so bright and dazzling. You must not look directly into the sun because this could be very harmful to your eyes.

Where do rainbows come from?

Some days it is rainy and sunny at the same time. The white light of the sun, which is made up of all the colors of the rainbow, sometimes passes through raindrops. When the light passes through and comes out again, the colors separate. They shine across the sky like a great arch. You cannot catch a rainbow because it is made of light.

Where do rainbows go when you don't see them?

Rainbows only appear if the sun shines and it rains at the same time. As soon as the rain stops, the rainbow disappears because there are no longer any raindrops to reflect the sun.

Why is the sky blue?

The air is full of very tiny pieces of dust. When the sun shines on them, the air appears blue.

Why are faraway mountains blue?

Take a look at the mountains far away. If you do not live near mountains, look at houses that are far away. They look slightly blue, yet they are not really blue. It is the air in front of them that seems blue because the sunlight is reflected as blue.

Why is the sun sometimes red?

You have learned that sunlight contains all the colors of the rainbow. Some evenings in good weather, tiny specks in the air block out the blue color. But the sun still has a lot of red and appears red in color.

The earth

Where did the earth come from?

The earth did not always exist. At the beginning of the world, there was hardly anything in the sky. Then the stars were formed. Around one special star, there were lots of tiny specks of dust. Over time, the specks joined together to form a huge ball. The ball is the earth. The special star is the sun.

Have there always been people on earth?

Scientists think that for a long time there were no plants, animals, or people on earth. Then very slowly the first plants and animals appeared on land and in the sea. Much later, people appeared on the earth.

Are there a lot of countries in the world?

Yes, there are many countries in the world —hot ones and cold ones, countries where it seldom rains, and countries where it rains each day. Some countries are huge, and some are tiny. Landscapes and the people of various countries differ, too.

How do you know when you have gone from one country to another or from one state to another?

In your house, each room is separate because of its walls. You know when you have gone into another room because you are on the other side of the wall. Different countries or states are sometimes divided from one another by the sea, a river, or a mountain range. This is not always the case, however. Sometimes a sign may be the only way to know if you have crossed a border into a different country or state.

Is it easy to go from one country or state to another?

Have you ever gone to another country or state on vacation? When countries or states are right next to each other, it is easy to travel to them by car. Some people live on islands that are completely surrounded by water with no bridges anywhere. These people have to take boats or planes to travel.

What is a continent? A continent is a mass of land. There are six continents on the earth. The rest of the earth is covered with water and a few islands.

Are there countries where nobody lives? No. Each country contains people. There are some countries, however, that have only a few families or some shepherds. These people live in deserts, mountains, or forests. Their daily existence can be very hard.

Are there still unknown countries? There are no countries left to be discovered. Explorers have been studying and making maps of the world for a long time. There are writings about and maps of every country in the world. However, there is still little information available about countries that are very hot or very cold.

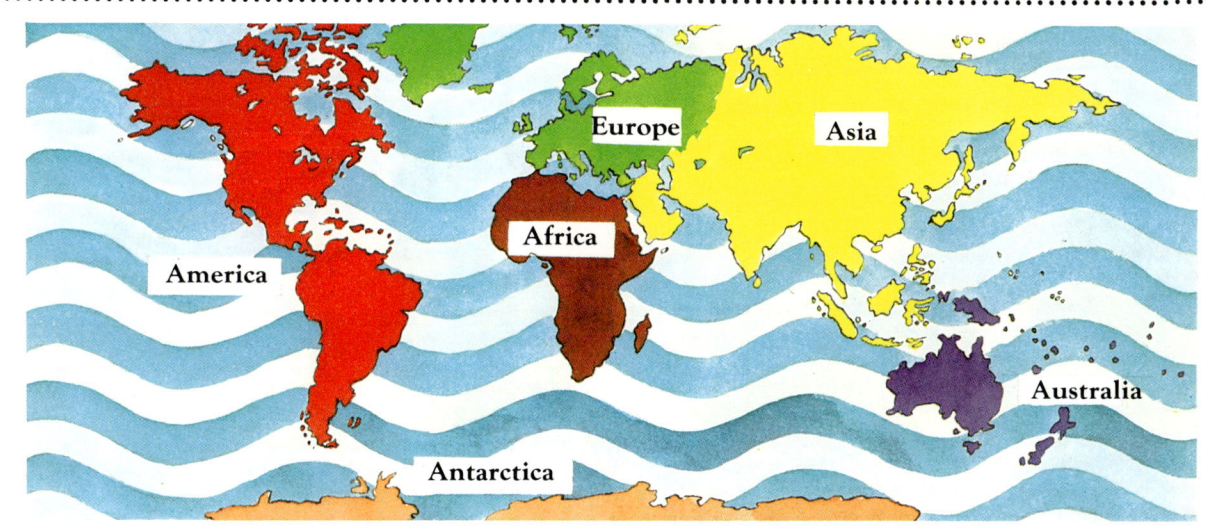

What shape is the earth?

The earth is not flat or square although it may seem that way. The earth is round and shaped like an enormous ball.

Why can't I see that the earth is round?

Balloons are round. But if you put a balloon up close to your eyes, it no longer looks round. In the same way, when you look at the earth, it looks flat. You are too close to it to see that the earth is round. The astronauts are the only people who have personally viewed the earth from far enough away to see that it is round.

Is there an underside to the earth?

If you were to see a caterpillar crawling around an apple on a tree, you can watch it crawl underneath the apple. The caterpillar doesn't realize it is underneath the apple because it can always feel the apple beneath its feet. People are like the caterpillar. The earth is always below your feet no matter where you are. But the earth is as round as an apple, and people live all over its surface.

33

How does the earth stay in the sky?

A spider in its web stays in the air because it is held there by tiny threads that make up its web. No threads are needed to keep the earth in the sky. The earth, stars, and the planets stay in the air by an invisible force called gravity.

Could the earth ever fall down?

No. Gravity, which keeps the earth in the sky, is very strong and it never stops.

Are there other earths in the sky?

The earth is a planet. There are several other planets in the sky. The earth has air and water which allow plants, animals, and humans to live. On the other known planets, there is neither air nor water. Therefore, life, as we know it, cannot exist.

How do I stay on the ground?

If you jump up high in the air, you will always come back down to the ground. Gravity pulls you back.

How do birds stay in the sky?

If birds stopped moving their wings up and down, they would fall to the ground just like a ball that is kicked up in the air returns to you. Airplanes would fall if they did not have engines. Gravity stops things from moving away from the earth.

How do soap bubbles stay in the air?

Soap bubbles don't have wings or engines yet they stay in the air. Bubbles can stay in the air because they are so light that gravity doesn't pull them down to the earth. They weigh so little that they usually burst before they get close enough to the ground to be affected by gravity. Feathers are also very light and can be seen floating through the air.

37

What is it like at the center of the earth?

A long time ago, the earth was formed from tiny specks of dust that joined together. This dust is packed together very tightly. The earth's center is so tightly packed that it is very hot. It is so hot that the large area surrounding the core has melted into a huge mass of liquid rock. It looks like the lava that flows from an erupting volcano.

Are there caves that reach the center of the earth?

There are caves so deep that you can travel through them by boat or train. The earth is so much deeper, however, that these caves are like tiny holes in the surface. There are no caves that reach all the way to the earth's center.

Can I dig a hole to the center of the earth?

No. Scientists have drilled a very deep hole in the earth in order to study its center. They put a very long tube under the sea to try to reach the core of the earth. But the earth is so huge that they could not drill deep enough.

39

Is it true that the earth turns like a top?

Yes, the earth turns completely around once each day. Each year, it travels once around the sun. In the sky, everything is turning; but you would need special instruments and a lot of time to notice this. Scientists have discovered that all the stars circle around each other.

Will the earth ever stop turning?

The earth will never stop turning because it is too big and too heavy. The sun and stars will always turn, too.

If the earth is turning, why don't I feel dizzy?

You don't feel the earth turning around and get dizzy because you have become used to it from the day you were born. Every day you turn with the earth without noticing it.

41

The sky

How do airplanes fly?

If the wind blows through your room and lifts up a piece of paper, it will carry the paper along. The same thing happens with an airplane. Air rushes under the wings to lift the plane up. A plane is very heavy, however, and it needs something more. An airplane has engines to make it move very fast so that a large amount of air passes under its wings.

Does the sky touch the earth?

When you are traveling down the highway, the trees in the distance seem to touch each other. As you get close to the trees, you can see that this is not true. From a distance, it seems as if the blue sky touches the earth, but it really does not.

43

Are there any mountains higher than the sky?

No, but some mountains are so tall that they rise above the clouds. Airplanes can fly over the highest mountains because the sky stretches far above the mountains.

What is beyond the sky?

The sky is not like a ceiling. You cannot go above it, behind it, or through it to the other side. It goes on forever. There is always more and more sky filled with stars.

Can the sky fall down?

A long, long time ago people were afraid that the sky would fall, but that is impossible. All the stars and planets in the sky are held there by gravity which never stops working.

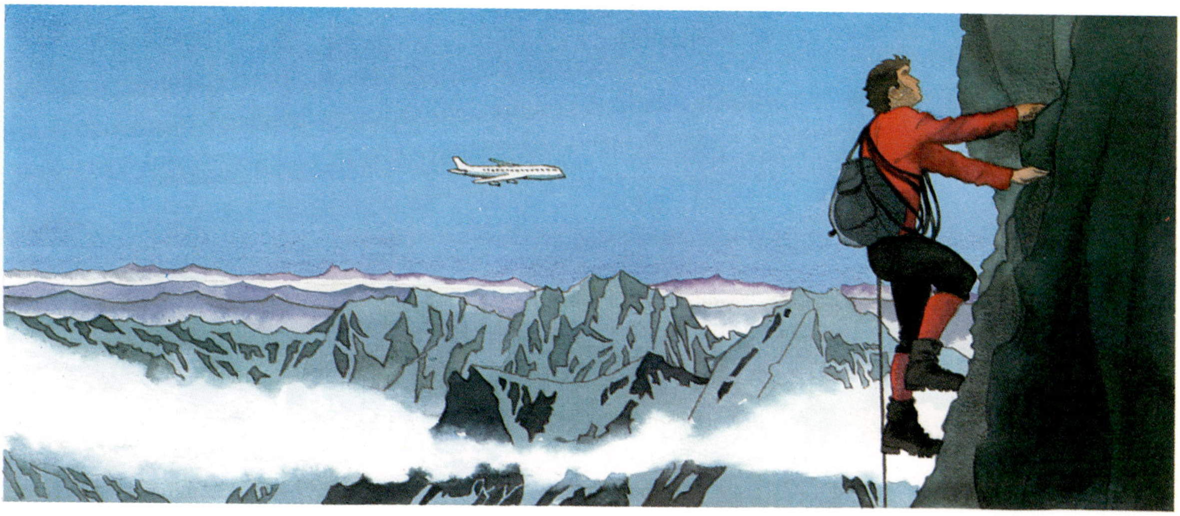

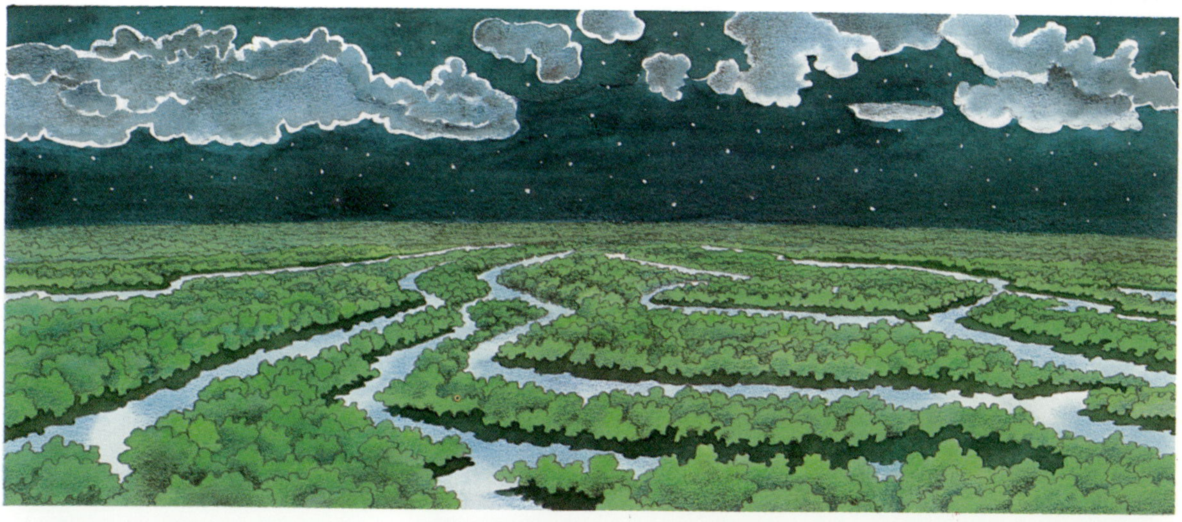

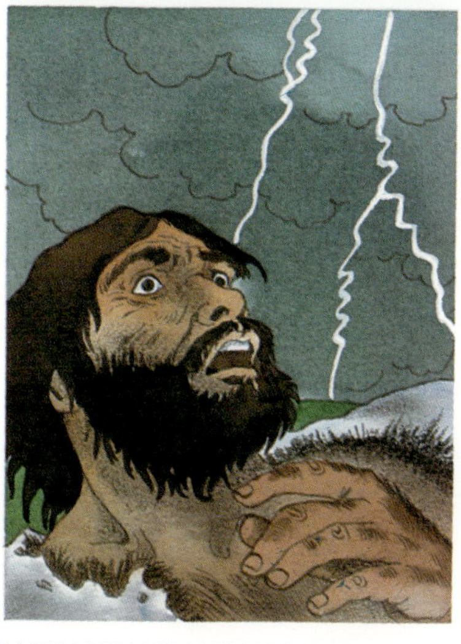

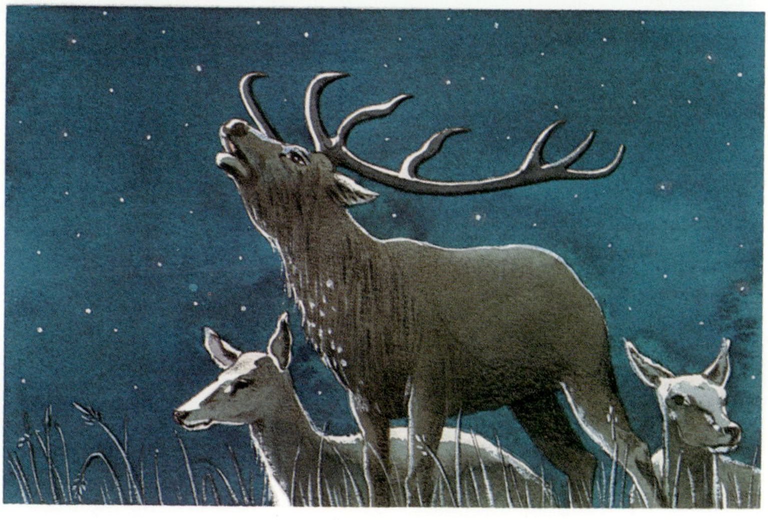

Where does the sun go when it sets?

At night after the sun goes down, you go to sleep. Does the sun go to bed, too? Does it fall into a deep hole or hide behind mountains? It doesn't do any of these things. It is still shining even at night, but you can't see it. The earth is an enormous ball that is always turning. When it is dark outside, it means that the area of the earth where you are has turned away from the sun.

How does night come?

When the sun is shining on the part of the earth where you are, it is daytime. It becomes nighttime as the earth turns farther and farther away from the sun. When it is dark where you are, it is light in other countries.

Does the night pass quickly?

During the day, you do a lot of things. You get up, eat, work, and play. The day lasts long. Nights are almost as long, but you don't notice it because you are asleep.

47

Why does the sun give us light?

Birthday candles on your cake don't give off much light. But think how great a light there would be from an entire mountain of candles. The sun is bigger than all the mountains put together, and it has a stronger light than any other light we know.

What is the sun like?

The sun is a huge ball that burns brightly in the sky. It is much bigger than the earth, but it looks small because it is so far away.

Can the sun be put out?

When a building is on fire, the fire department uses water to put the fire out. The sun is so big and hot that all the water in the world could not put it out. The sun is so hot that no one could even get near it.

49

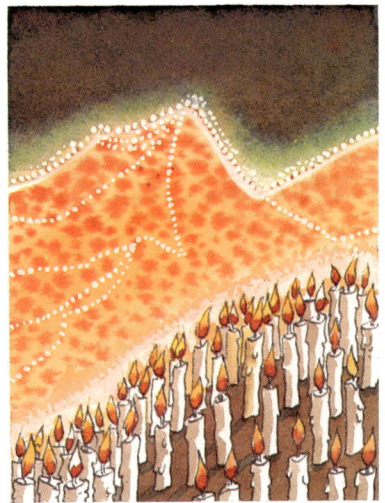

What is a full moon?

The moon is a big ball in the sky. The moon does not have light of its own. It is lit up by the sun. Every twenty-eight days, the sun lights the front side of the moon. This makes the moon look big, bright, full, and round.

Why does the moon change its shape?

Sometimes the sun shines on only part of the moon. The rest of it is in shadow. In a cycle of twenty-eight days, the moon changes from a full moon to a thin crescent. Think of the sun as an electric light bulb and the moon as a ping pong ball. As you move the ball around, some areas of the ball are in light, and some are in shadow.

Which is bigger, the moon or the sun?

It's hard to tell how big things are in the sky by just looking at them because they are so far away. The farther away something is, the smaller it looks. The moon can look the same size as the sun, but the sun is really much bigger. If the sun were even farther away, it would look like a tiny star. Faraway lights on the highway look smaller than the ones that are near.

51

Do clouds touch the moon?

On some evenings, clouds cover the moon and we cannot see it. As the clouds move, the moon may reappear but then disappear again behind more clouds. The clouds and the moon never touch. The moon is much farther away in space than the clouds. The clouds simply block the view of the moon at times, just like a passing truck can block the view of the mountains.

Can airplanes fly to the moon?

Have you ever eaten a caramel apple? Just like the apple is surrounded by a layer of caramel, the earth is surrounded by a layer of air. No air surrounds the moon. Ordinary airplanes cannot fly in outer space to the moon because they must always have air to operate.

Can rockets go to the moon?

Yes, rockets or spaceships can go to the moon because they are more powerful than ordinary airplanes. They can be launched high into the sky and travel in outer space. Astronauts have traveled to the moon in spaceships.

53

What is it like inside a spaceship?

Spaceships can be very tall—as tall as a building. At the top of a spaceship is a small room called a capsule where the astronauts travel. The engine and the fuel make up the rest of the spaceship.

Why must astronauts wear special clothing?

Inside the capsule, there is air to breathe just like on earth. But outside the capsule, astronauts must wear special helmets to help them breathe because there is no air in outer space. It can also become very cold or hot in space, and the uniforms protect them.

Why do astronauts float in space?

When an astronaut walks in outer space, he or she floats like a feather because there is no gravity. People have no weight when there is no gravity, and they float. Astronauts can again walk when they reach surfaces where there is gravity.

55

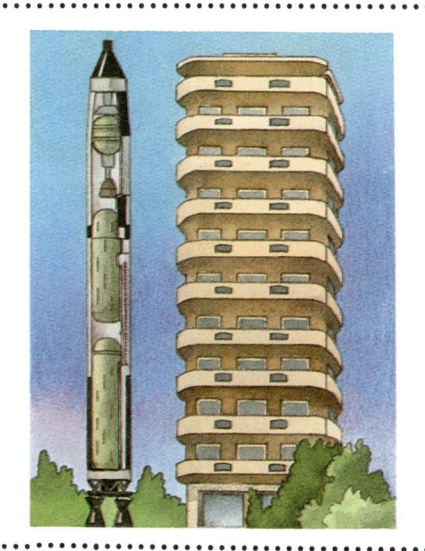

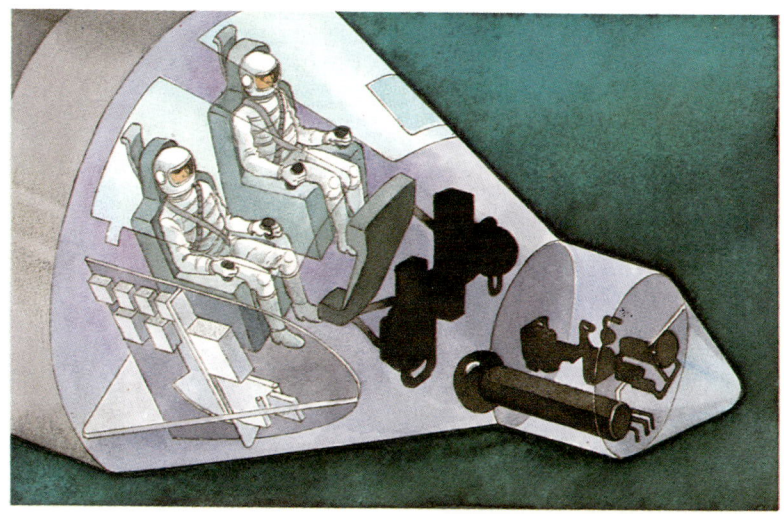

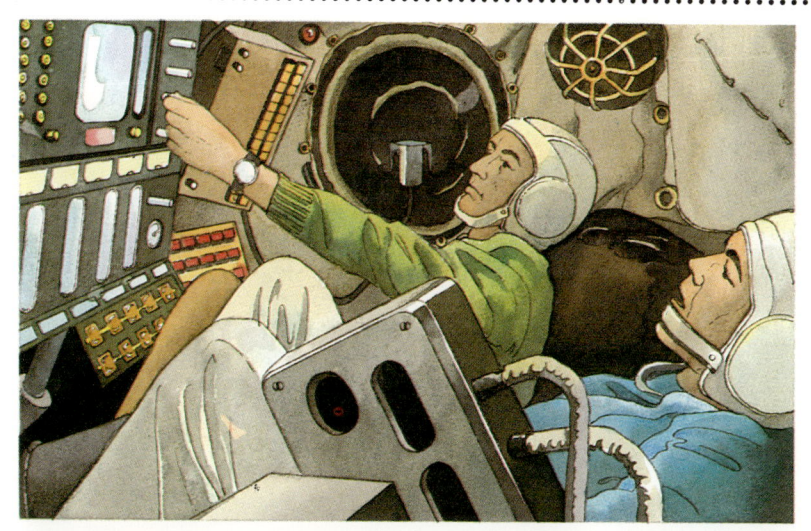

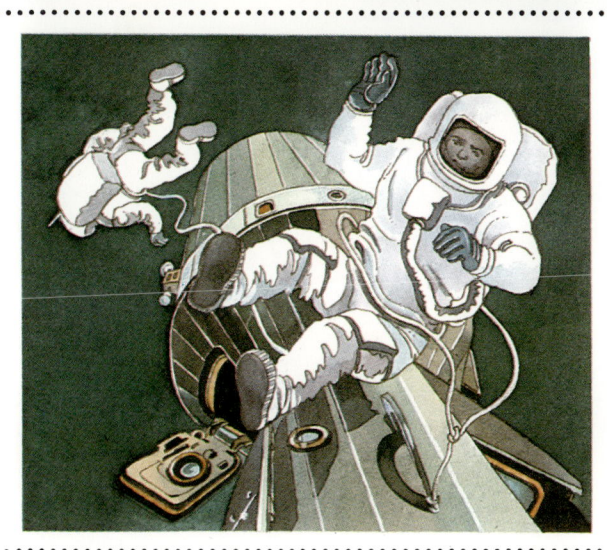

What is the man in the moon?

There are markings on the moon which can look like a face with two big eyes and a mouth. Although this is known as the "man in the moon," there isn't really a man. The marks are just the empty plains on the moon.

Are there mountains on the moon?

Scientists can see mountains and large holes called craters when they look at the moon through powerful telescopes. No living creatures—people or animals—have been seen on the moon.

Are there any plants on the moon?

Astronauts have been to the moon and brought back stones and dust for study. They did not find any plants, not even a single blade of grass. Nothing can grow on the moon because there is no air or water.

57

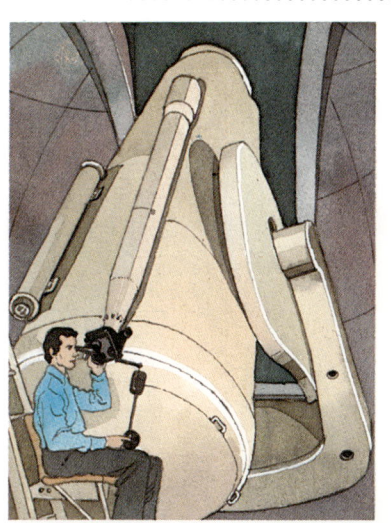

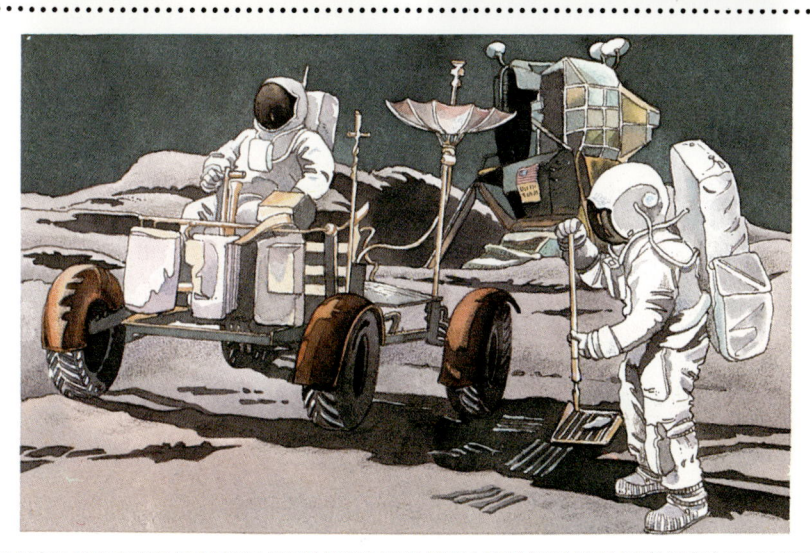

What are stars?

Stars look smaller than the sun, but they are really huge round burning balls. Some are even larger than the sun. The sun appears bigger because it is closer. The stars are so far away that you cannot tell their real shape. You just see tiny, bright dots.

Do stars disappear during the day?

When it is dark, you can see a desklamp shine. In the daylight, you can't see that light bulb shine because the sun is so strong. You don't see stars shine during the day because the light from the sun is so strong. We see the stars at night because there is no sunlight.

Can we ever reach the stars?

It is currently impossible to travel to the stars. They are too far away, and it would take longer than a lifetime to reach them. The stars have to be enjoyed from the earth.

59

Glossary

astronaut—a person who travels beyond the earth's atmosphere (pp. 52, 54)

capsule—a small room at the top of a spaceship where the astronauts sit (p. 54)

continent—a large mass of land (p. 30)

craters—large holes on the moon (p. 56)

full moon—an occurrence every twenty-eight days when the sun lights the entire front side of the moon (p. 50)

gravity—the attraction on a planet or the moon for things at or near its surface (p. 34)

lightning—giant sparks of electricity in the sky (p. 18)

man in the moon—markings on the moon which can make it look like a face (p. 56)

meteorologists—scientists that study the atmosphere and predict the weather (p. 20)

rainbow—a great, colorful arch made of light created when sunlight passes through raindrops (p. 22)

spaceship—a vehicle designed to operate outside the earth's atmosphere (p. 54)

stars—huge round burning balls in the sky, some even larger than the sun (p. 58)

thunder—a loud noise caused by the quick movement of air when lightning flashes across the sky (p. 18)

volcano—an opening in the crust of the earth from which liquid rock and gases explode (p. 38)

Index

airplanes 42, 52
astronauts 32, 52
birds 36
birthday 48
boats 28
bridges 28
bubbles 36
capsule 54
clouds 8, 14
colors 24
continent 30
countries 28, 30
craters 56
dust 56
earth 32, 34, 40
electricity 18
explorers 30
feathers 36
fire 48
forecasting 20
full moon 50
grass 58
gravity 34, 36, 44
islands 30
landscapes 28
lightning 18

man in the moon 56
meteorologists 20
moon 50
mountains 16, 44
night 46
planet 34, 44
plants 26
rain 16
rainbow 22
sewers 20
shepherds 30
sky 44
smoke 12
snow 16
spaceship 54
stars 44
steam 12
stones 56, 58
sun, setting 46
sunlight 22, 48
telescopes 56
thunder 18
vacation 28
volcano 38
weather 20
wind 8